The EYE Book

by Theo.
LeSieg

Illustrated by

Roy McKie

A Bright & Early Book

Eye   Eyes

My eyes
My eyes

His eyes
His eyes

Wink eye
Wink eye

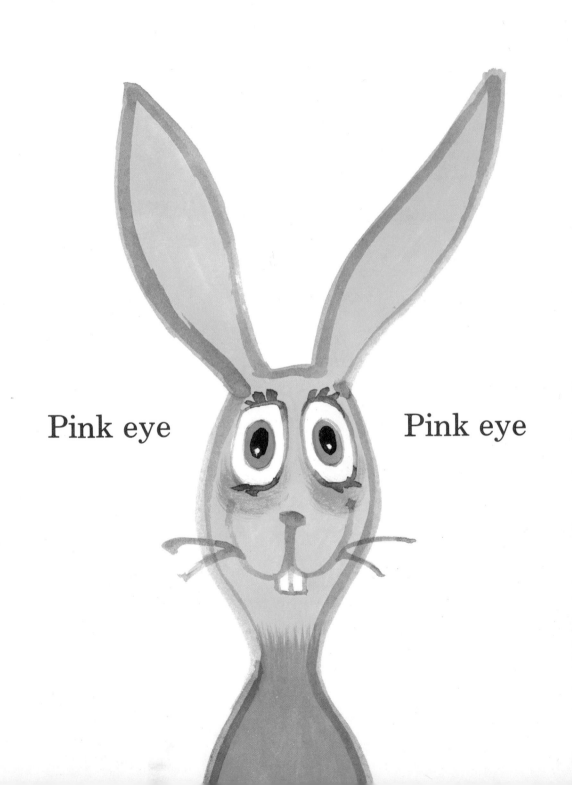

Pink eye

Pink eye

My eyes see.

His eyes see.

I see him.

And he sees me.

Our eyes see blue.

Our eyes see red.

They see a bird.

They see a bed.

They see the sun.

They see the moon.

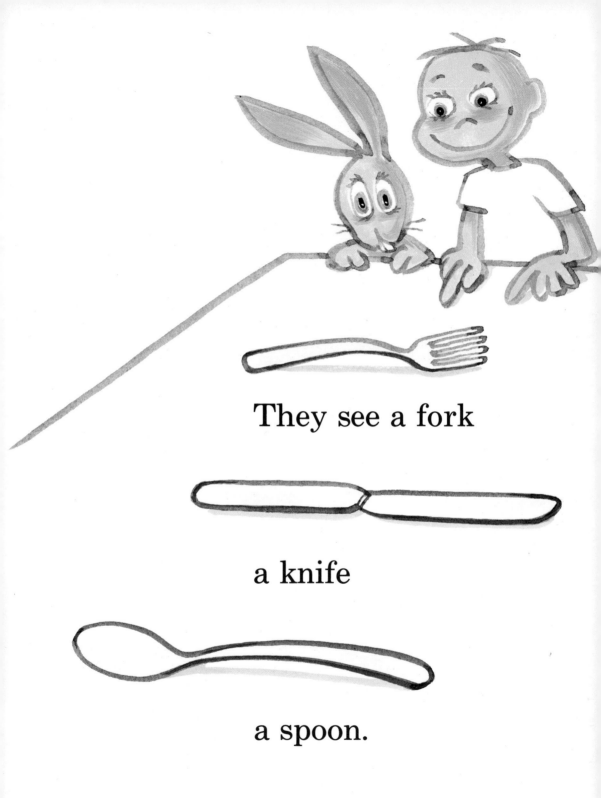

They see a fork

a knife

a spoon.

They see a girl.

They see a man . . .

a boy

a horse

an old tin can.

They look down holes.

They look up poles.

Our eyes see trees.

They look at clocks.

They look at bees.

They look at socks.

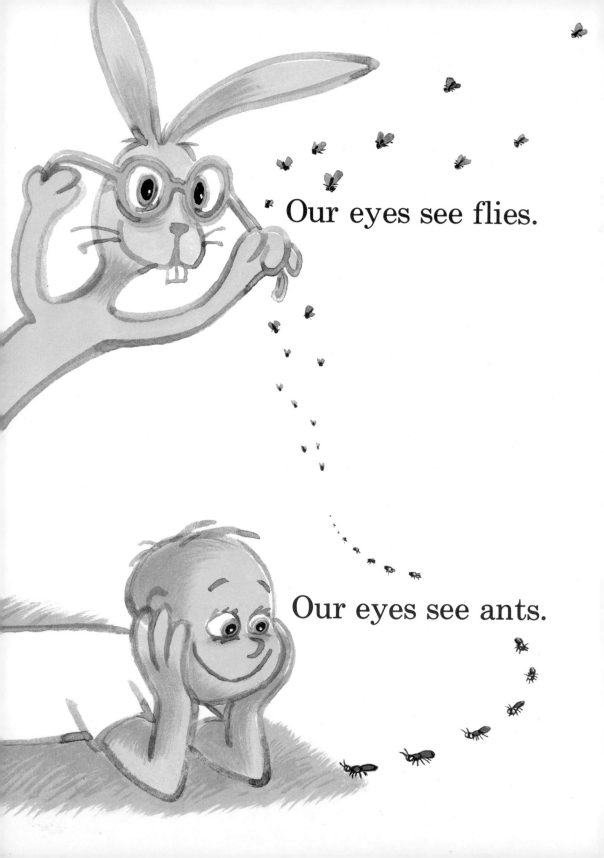

Our eyes see flies.

Our eyes see ants.

Sometimes they see
pink under pants.

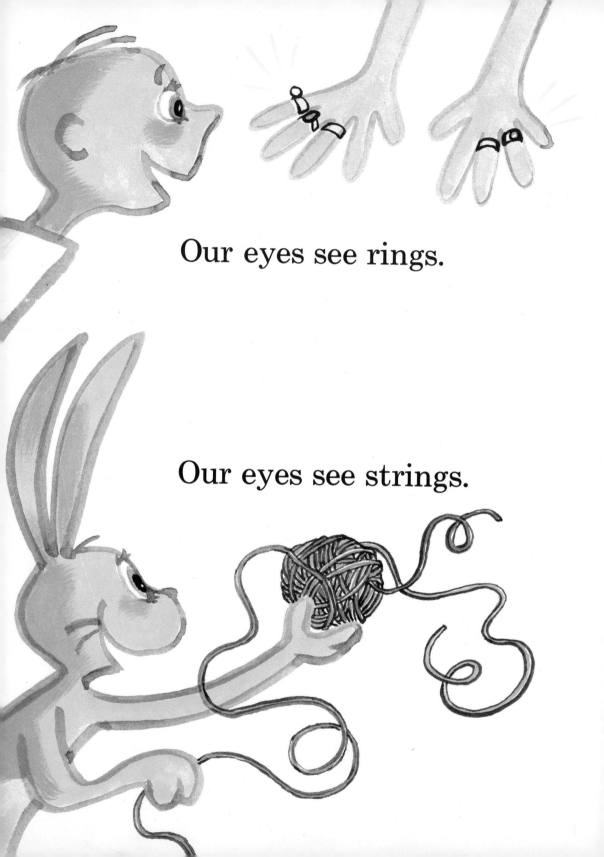

Our eyes see rings.

Our eyes see strings.

They see
so many, many things!

So many things!

Like rain

and pie . . .

and dogs

and airplanes
in the sky!

And so we say,
"Hooray for eyes!
Hooray, hooray, hooray . . .

. . . for eyes!"